# A Brotherly Bother

# HAVE YOU READ?

# PIP STREET

## A Brotherly Bother

### Jo Simmons

Illustrated by Steve Wells

**SCHOLASTIC**

First published in the UK in 2014 by Scholastic Children's Books
An imprint of Scholastic Ltd
Euston House, 24 Eversholt Street
London, NW1 1DB, UK
Registered office: Westfield Road, Southam, Warwickshire, CV47 0RA
SCHOLASTIC and associated logos are trademarks and/or registered
trademarks of Scholastic Inc.

ISBN 978 1 407 13284 6

A CIP catalogue record for this book is available
from the British Library.

Printed and bound by CPI Group (UK) Ltd, Croydon, CR0 4YY
Papers used by Scholastic Children's Books are made from
wood grown in sustainable forests.

1 3 5 7 9 10 8 6 4 2

www.scholastic.co.uk
www.visitpipstreet.com

For Zoe,

with huge thanks for all the fun,

support and *Bake Off* chats

Jo Simmons

Oi Ned – stop watching telly

and play some guitar!

Steve Wells

# 1
## Sleigh Bells Ring

Here we are on Pip Street once again, boys and girls. My, it's good to be back!

The sun is bathing the houses in afternoon golden goodness and look! Someone is coming... It's a man on a penny-farthing. How quaint! And heading up the street behind him are two more characters.

1

One is boy shaped, the other is small and springy and jumping about. Of course, it can only be Bobby Cobbler and his tiddly wee mate Imelda Small returning home from an afternoon's chaffinch spotting. Hoorah! Let's join them.

The two children were passing Café Coffee when they stopped suddenly and listened. There was a sound. An unusual sound: bells! Not bing-bonging church bells, but lovely tinkling bells.

"Santa!" cried Imelda, looking up at the sky.

"No!" said Bobby, pointing up the street. "Look!"

Speeding round the corner of Pip Street was an amazing vehicle. It looked like a chariot from Roman times – with bells on! A tall man with a thick moustache was sitting holding the reins, but instead of horses pulling it, there were five huge dogs with white and brown fur – and these dogs were racing towards Bobby and Imelda.

"Whoa boys," shouted the driver, and the chariot-sleigh-thing stopped alongside the children.

Bobby and Imelda stared, wide-eyed.

"Impressive, aren't they?" said the man, nodding towards his dogs. "Viper, Storm, Clamp, Bovver

4

and Reggie. They just love to pull. Born to do it."

The dogs were fidgeting and whining, eager to run again, their tongues hanging out like dribbly ham slices.

"Are they huskies?" asked Bobby.

*"Huskies?"* said the man, looking shocked, as if Bobby had asked if they were porcupines or kittens or ladybirds.

"No, boy!" said the man. "Malamutes! Alaskan malamutes. Tough dogs. Strong, brave and loyal.

5

Unlike most people I know..."

The man chuckled darkly to himself.

"My legs aren't so good since I had my accident," the moustache man continued, "but my dogs keep me up and running, so to speak."

"Do you live near here?" asked Bobby, just to be polite. He couldn't help himself – he was polite through and through, like a stick of rock with "POLITE" written inside.

"No," said the man. "But I'm on a little fracking mission. I find oil and gas underground and sell it for lots of money. People need oil and gas to heat their homes, among many other things. That's why I'm here. I believe there is natural gas in the stones under Pip Street and probably all around this neighbourhood. We are standing on a fortune!

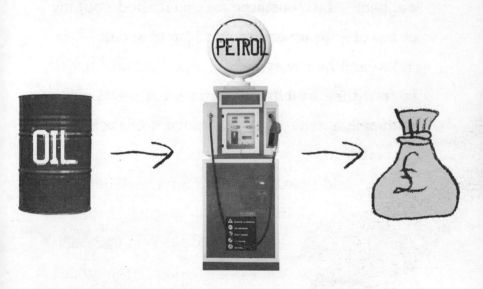

I just need to crack the ground - BOOM! - and squeeze all the gas out."

The man stared at the children.

"If I squeezed you, would gas come out of you, too, do you suppose?" he asked, and then he laughed; a big, booming laugh, loud enough to be heard on Dip Street and Chip Street, too. The children gulped nervously.

"Now then friends," the man went on. "Does a gentleman by the name of Richard Keiths still live at number 8?"

"Yep," said Imelda, pointing up the road.

"That's exactly where he lives."

Bobby winced. Imelda, known for blurting, had blurted again, but Bobby felt uneasy. Why did this stranger want to check where Mr Keiths lived?

The man stared hard at Mr Keith's house.

"Good," he said, nodding slowly. "That's my house, you see. Or it will be, in time!"

The children gawped, but before they could question the man, he shouted "Mush!" and the dogs took off, barking and slobbering. The chariot-sleigh-thing raced away.

"Who was *that*?" said Imelda. "And what was he driving? And what in the name of spangles was he on about? That's Mr Keiths' house, plain and simple, not his."

9

"I don't understand either," said Bobby. "He looked familiar, though, didn't he?"

Imelda shrugged. She was too dazzled by the creepy man on his weird vehicle. *What would you even call that kind of sleigh crossed with a chariot?* Imelda was thinking. Who knows? Let's just call it a crazy sleigh and be done.

The crazy sleigh had been spotted by other Pip Street residents, too. Mrs Rhubarb, the actor who lived next door to Bobby, and Imelda's big, tall brother

Nathan had heard the bells and peeped out from their front room windows. Nathan frowned and pulled the brown dressing gown that he always wore tightly around him.

Once the woofing had died down, Conkers, Bobby's black cat, tiptoed cautiously on to the pavement to double-check that the dogs had gone, his tail puffed up like a frightened chipolata.

11

Jeff the Chalk also came to join the children. He looked worried. Dogs and their mess were Jeff's number-one no-no. He devoted heaps of time to chalking messages around dog poos, to remind

the dog owners to clean them up. Naturally, he had a bad feeling about those huge mutts.

"Bet they leave a lot of poo around the streets, Jeff," said Bobby. Jeff frowned hard, his pale, oblong face looking like a serious pitta bread.

"I can't imagine that man hopping out of his vehicle to clean the poos up, either," chalked Jeff on the notebook he kept in his top pocket.

"He was talking about finding gas under the street," said Bobby. "And he said Mr Keiths' house was his."

Jeff frowned even harder and then he chalked the word BAD and underlined it three times, just to emphasise its badness.

The man's presence on Pip Street was indeed bad, and would get badder still. But I'm rushing ahead. Let's calm down a minute. It's time to start another chapter...

# 2
## Pegasus Kaput

The next morning, Bobby walked down to the newsagents, This Is The News!, to pick up the local newspaper, *The Daily Wotsit*.

He read the headlines as he ambled back up the street:

**MAN WHO LOST GLASSES**
**FOUND WANDERING UP MOTORWAY**

**CITY'S BUS DRIVERS CALL FOR COMEDY
HORNS TO BE FITTED ON ALL BUSES**

**LOCAL QUICHE LOVER ADMITS:
"I ATE 68 QUICHES IN ONE DAY!"**

*Squeezy satsumas*, Bobby was thinking. *Sixty-eight quiches are enough to make you...*

"Bobby!" shouted a voice. "Over here!"

The voice belonged to Imelda, who was outside Richard Keiths' house. Mr Keiths was sitting on his mobility scooter, Pegasus, next to the lovely old Pearly Oak tree that grew in his front garden. His grey skin was looking slightly less grey in the early morning sun, but even so, he looked properly cheesed off.

15

"Mr Keiths is sadder than a Sunday evening," explained Imelda.

Mr Keiths rubbed his stubbly chin and sighed.

"She's quit on me," he said.

"Who?" asked Bobby.

"Pegasus," said Mr Keiths. "Won't start. Won't move. I'm stuck here."

Pegasus was Mr Keiths only means of getting about. He liked to drive his scooter super-fast up and down the street.

"It's an apostrophe, isn't it, Bobby?" said Imelda.

"Catastrophe," said Bobby.

"Oh, right," said Imelda. "How will Mr Keiths get to the Co-op to buy those readily salted crisps he loves?"

Just then a white van pulled up outside the house, with music blaring from its stereo. A tall man wearing overalls hopped down from the driver's seat.

"All right, Granddad?" he said.

It was Tommy – Mr Keiths' grandson and ace mechanic.

Mr Keiths introduced Tommy to the children. He smiled at them, and then quickly marched over to Pegasus. He began checking over the engine, tapping and tinkering with a spanner he kept behind his ear.

"What's the problem, then?" said Mr Keiths, when Tommy finally looked up.

Tommy wiped his spanner on his overalls and sucked in a long breath.

"The fuel crisper's burnt out," Tommy said. "The combobulator is damaged and I think the big matrix is about to go, too."

Mr Keiths nodded, taking in the serious news.

"Can you fix it?" he asked Tommy.

"Sure," said Tommy, slipping the spanner behind his ear. "But the parts are expensive."

"How much?" asked Mr Keiths, his eyes narrowing.

"I'll find out and call you," said Tommy, hopping back into his van.

The children and their elderly friend watched the van drive away.

"Don't worry, Mr Keiths," said Bobby. "I'm sure Tommy can put Pegasus right and you'll be motoring around the neighbourhood again soon."

"Maybe," said Mr Keiths, rubbing his chin. "But parts cost. We're talking cash money. And cash money is what I don't have."

The children looked worried.

"Anyway," said Mr Keiths, with a glint in his eye. "Enough mobility misery. You kids coming over later to watch *How Much?*"

Bobby and Imelda beamed. *How Much?* was their new favourite programme. People brought their prized possessions to an expert called Carshalton Beeches and he told them how much they were worth. Sometimes it was loads and the people would shout "How much?" excitedly. Bobby and Imelda and Mr Keiths loved it when that happened and would shout "How much? How much?" at each other lots of times and have a right old laugh... Marvellous!

"We would *love* to come and watch *How Much?* with you," said Bobby. "I'll bring popcorn."

# 3
## How Much?

Later that day, Bobby and Imelda went down to Mr Keiths' house with a big bowl of popcorn for a matey TV-watching session.

*How Much?* had just started and was shaping up to be a cracking episode. A man had brought along a knobbly wooden thing which he had found up his granny's chimney, and it turned

22

out to be a genuine Tudor cheese grater. The expert, Carshalton Beeches, said it was worth £150.

"How much?" said the man.

"How much?" shouted Bobby.

"How much?" roared Imelda, popcorn erupting out of her mouth as if it were a popcorn volcano.

The children laughed and laughed. Mr Keiths smiled and nodded.

Next up was a lady from Surrey with a stuffed seagull in a glass case. Carshalton Beeches was looking at it when Mr Keiths' phone rang.

"Hey Tommy," said Mr Keiths down the phone. "You got the low-down on the parts for Pegasus? What's the damage?"

Mr Keiths listened to Tommy. On the TV, the expert was examining the seagull.

"I think this is no ordinary seagull," said Carshalton Beeches. "I think it is actually the famous sailor Admiral Lord Knockerbox's pet seagull, Derrick. And this fine bird is worth quite a bit, I should say. Around £250."

"How much?" blurted the lady.

"How much?" shrieked Bobby and Imelda, laughing.

"How much?" spluttered Mr Keiths down the phone to Tommy.

The children turned quickly to look at Mr Keiths, their smiles fading.

Mr Keiths hung up and rubbed his chin.

"All those parts for Pegasus are going to cost £500," he said.

"How much?" said Bobby and Imelda. Only this time they weren't laughing.

"I don't have £500. Not now, not ever," said Mr Keiths. "Had a feeling repairs might get expensive, but if I can't fix my scooter, I can't live

25

here. I need my wheels. Without them, I'll have to leave. Maybe move in with Tommy."

"But we can go to the Co-op for you, Mr Keiths, for all your bits and bobbins," protested Imelda. "We can help!"

"Thanks," said Mr Keiths. "Kind of you, but that's no solution. I can't live like that – stranded! The only solution is cash – but where is an old dude like me going to find £500?"

"If only you were as rich as that man we saw yesterday," said Imelda. "The weirdy guy with the crazy sleigh who said there is gas and money right under the street."

Mr Keiths went pale. (Pale grey, that is.)

"This man – did he have a big bushy

moustache?" Mr Keiths asked.

"Yes!" said Imelda. "Like a hamster was asleep under his nostrils!"

"Walter!" Mr Keiths whispered.

"Who's Walter?" asked Bobby.

"Walter William Keiths," said Mr Keiths slowly. "He's my brother, technically, although he's no brother to me really. He's a hard man. Greedy. Selfish. Rich, too, as you spotted, Imelda."

Bobby and Imelda looked nervously at one another and then Mr Keiths explained how he had one brother, Walter, who was younger than him. Walter's job was finding oil and gas all over the world, and because we all need oil and gas every day, Walter could sell it for lots of money. His leg had been damaged in a mining accident years ago, but that did not stop him, and even though he was super-rich, he was always searching for new oil fields and gas buried underground, so he could make more millions.

"So that is why he was talking about squeezing gas out from under Pip Street," said Bobby.

28

"But surely he can't do that? This is a quiet street with houses and shops. How's he going to dig about for gas while we all live here?"

"Walter has a way of doing just whatever he likes, and I'm afraid that if he finds gas here, he won't rest until he's torn up the whole street to get at it," said Mr Keiths, looking serious.

"There's more bad news, too, kids," Mr Keiths went on. "I'm afraid that, because of me and my house, he has a claim to the street which will make it easier for him to start digging."

Bobby looked bothered and then said: "Walter did say your house was his house. . ."

"Which just has to be bonkers, doesn't it?" piped up Imelda.

"Our mum left this house to me," explained Mr Keiths. "But only so long as I live here. After that, it becomes Walter's. I had hoped he was hundreds of miles away. Seems he has come home just in time to benefit from Pegasus breaking down."

Bobby frowned a massive frown. Pegasus breaking down and making Mr Keiths leave Pip Street would be bad enough. Now, there was a chance that Walter with his huge dogs might move in. Even worse, Walter planned to dig up Mr Keiths' garden in search of gas. And if he found gas there – then what? He might dig up the whole of Pip Street to get his greedy hands on it and make money. Everyone could lose their homes!

It seems Jeff had been right when he had

chalked those fateful letters just the day before.

BAD!

# 4
## Hey Good Looking

The children left Mr Keiths' house feeling bothered. They didn't want their old friend to move from the street. Richard Keiths had lived here for so many years – he was a Pip Street legend. Besides, Bobby and Imelda would miss watching *How Much?* with him; miss seeing him zipping about on his mobility scooter, scattering pedestrians all over the place; and Bobby would

miss the electric guitar lessons that Mr Keiths gave him. On top of that, they just felt sorry for him, like the nice, caring children they were.

"It must be hard when you can't walk very well and have to rely on a scooter," said Bobby, in his thoughtful way.

"Yes, I mean, I absolutely love walking, and all the other things that go with it," said Imelda.

"Like jumping, spinning around, hopping and running really fast. Mr Keiths can't do any of those, the poor old turnip."

"If only we could raise the £500 Mr Keiths needs to repair Pegasus," said Bobby. "Then he would be able to stay on the street and Walter could not move in."

"But how? £500 is a big lot," said Imelda. "It's not the sort of money you find down the back of the sofa. Not unless you have a very rich sofa."

The children arrived at Bobby's house and sat in the kitchen, distracted and sad. Bobby flicked through *The Daily Wotsit*, past the adverts for sofa shops and a notice about a local car boot sale this coming Saturday, until he noticed this:

34

# DOES YOUR CAT HAVE THE MIAOW FACTOR?

FISH LUMPS CAT FOOD IS LOOKING FOR A NEW KITTY STAR!

SEND YOUR PHOTOS IN NOW.

THE BEST CAT WILL APPEAR ON EVERY PACKET OF FISH LUMPS AND WIN £150! WINNER ANNOUNCED ON FRIDAY.

Bobby read the advert several times.

*Mr Keiths needs cash*, thought Bobby, *and cash is being offered here. For a cat with good looks. I know a cat with good—*

At that moment, Conkers leaped on to the table and lay there, looking majestic.

"Conkers," said Bobby. "Stay there. We have a beauty contest to enter."

# 5
# Who Is the Fairest Cat of All?

Without wasting a nanosecond, Bobby set about preparing Conkers for his photographs. Imelda called her brother Nathan, who was wearing his brown dressing gown as per usual, to help, too. The two Smalls held Conkers still, while Bobby fluffed out his tail with a hairbrush and polished his whiskers with a cotton pad.

37

"Imagine if Conkers wins all that money!" said
Imelda. "Just think of all the things you could buy
at **Gizmo World**."

**Gizmo World** was the electrical store at
the bottom of Pip Street, rammed with tempting
gadgets for young and old.

"No Imelda," said Bobby. "If Conkers wins, I'm going to give the £150 to Mr Keiths to help get Pegasus fixed."

"Good idea," said Nathan. "We want to keep Mr Keiths on the street and Walter off it."

"Exactly," said Bobby. "Mr Keiths has lived on Pip Street for as long as anyone can remember. It would not be the same without him."

"It would be a Mr Keiths desert," said Imelda, staring into the distance sadly.

"Plus, Walter moving on to Pip Street could be disastrous for all of us," Bobby continued. "Mr Keiths reckons he might flatten the whole street – all our homes! – and chuck us out. We cannot let that happen. So I thought maybe if we all tried, we could raise enough money; a sort of **Parts for Pegasus Appeal**."

"Oh Bobster," said Imelda. "You have a heart made of silver and gold and extra-sweet jam! What a super-tastic idea. I'll help. It's a good challenge, isn't it? I like a challenge and I most certainly do not like the idea of Walter moving here. I'm in!"

"Me, too," said Nathan.

The three friends shook hands, then Bobby began photographing his black cat and, with help from Nathan, he emailed the best shots over to the Fish Lumps factory at this address: prettykittycomp@fish-lumps.co.uk.

"The judges are mad as cheesecakes if they don't choose Conkers," said Imelda, admiring the photos.

"He may not win," said Bobby, sensibly. "Anyway, we won't find out for a few days. In the meantime, if we're going to fix Pegasus and keep Mr Keiths on the street, we need to think up more money-making ideas."

It was getting late, though, and the children felt too tired for brainwaves.

"Let's sleep on it tonight," said Bobby, "but tomorrow – think money!"

# 6

## Biccies and the Brown Dressing Gown

The next day was Wednesday, the day that almost always follows Tuesday. In the morning, bright and early, Bobby, Imelda and Nathan met outside on Pip Street and thought. And thought. And thought some more. They told Jeff the Chalk and little Dave Pasty, who lived at number 3, about the Appeal, and the friends began suggesting ideas for money-raising schemes.

"I could sell my Dad's Toby jug collection," suggested Dave.

But everyone said, no, that would get Dave into trouble.

"I could chalk the Mona Lisa on the pavement and charge people for a view," offered Jeff the Chalk. But no, that was too time-consuming. And what if it rained?

"I could do a sponsored stay awake!" said Imelda. But no, that was too tiring, and everyone knew how much Imelda enjoyed her sleep.

The friends batted more ideas around, then finally decided. Nathan would do a dressing-gown-athon. Friends and neighbours would

45

sponsor him to keep his dressing gown on for the rest of the week. Nathan was excited. He got started right away. Jeff, Dave, Imelda and Bobby decided to cook up the cash – as it were – by baking biscuits to sell at Café Coffee. They headed to Bobby's kitchen and began a baking session that lasted well into the evening.*

Mrs Rhubarb popped in later to offer her support. She wasn't much of a cook, but she had put on a new hat for the occasion, to keep everyone cheerful.

*Bobby and Imelda had come second in a crazy crumpet competition held a few months back – you can read about it in A Crumpety Calamity. These two really knew how to knock up a tasty teatime treat, yes sir.

The following morning, as Bobby and Imelda carried the biscuits down to Café Coffee, they noticed Mr Keiths, sitting in his front garden, his walking stick hooked over the arm of his chair.

"We have been baking," said Imelda, waving a choc-chip cookie at Mr Keiths. She was dressed as a chef, complete with tall hat and black and white checked trousers. "The money we make from selling these here biscuits is going into the **Parts for Pegasus Appeal**!"

"The what for what what?" asked Mr Keiths.

Imelda explained that Mr Keiths' Pip Street chums were raising money to get his mobility scooter fixed and keep him on – and Walter off – the street.

"That's kind," said Mr Keiths. "I don't know what to say."

A pink blush crept into his greyish cheeks, as if someone had rubbed a tiny bit of raspberry jam on them.

"Don't say anything," said Imelda. "Just keep believing. We'll get Pegasus fixed; just you see if we don't!"

Then Bobby and Imelda turned to walk down to Café Coffee with their biscuits, but their journey was stopped by a sound. Faint at first. Then louder. Then louder still. Then even louder. . .

The bells! The bells!

"Oh my perkins!" said Bobby. "It's Walter again!"

# 7
## Walter Again!

It certainly was Walter – again! Bobby and Imelda stood rooted to the spot as Nathan and Mrs Rhubarb rushed outside, just in time to see Viper, Storm, Clamp, Bovver and Reggie pulling the crazy sleigh around the corner of Pip Street. Walter called "Whoa", stopping the dogs outside Mr Keiths' house.

"Hello Walter," said Mr Keiths, standing up to greet his brother. "Been a while."

"Richard!" said Walter. "How are you keeping?"

"What do you want here, Walter?" asked Mr Keiths, leaning on his stick. "This is a peaceful street with cats on it. We don't want trouble or dogs or anything."

"Well, as I told these children here, I believe there may be gas right underneath this street," smiled Walter. "Even underneath my future home. So I wanted to get another look at the place."

Richard Keiths winced.

"This is no home of yours," he said, "until I have to leave, which I don't plan on doing any time soon."

"But Mr K," blurted Imelda. "What if you can't get Pegasus fixed?"

"Shhh," hissed Bobby. But it was too late. Walter had heard.

"Pegasus broken down has she?" asked Walter, a smile emerging from under his moustache and stretching across his rugged face. "Well, well.

Seems I came just in time. You're stuck, are you not, Richard, without your wheels? Should have got some dogs, brother – they *never* break down."

The dogs barked and licked each other's faces. Clamp jumped up and snatched a biscuit from Imelda's plate while Reggie did a little poo on the street. Poor Jeff went pale with shock when he saw this and had to sit on a garden wall.

"Perhaps Tommy will take you in?" continued Walter. "I, for one, think that is an excellent idea. . ."

"So you can help yourself to my house," said Mr Keiths, crossly.

"Ooh, more than that!" grinned Walter. "I

don't really care about this house, you see. I care about what lies beneath it, and I will flatten the whole house to get at it. In fact, I might just take down the entire street, too, so I can dig as I choose without any silly neighbours standing in my way!"

The neighbours gasped in shock. The two Keiths stared at each other in silence.

It seemed the brothers might never stop staring at each other;

as if they were having some kind of weird, on-street staring competition. But suddenly Walter glanced to his left, his attention caught by a movement. Conkers!

Bobby's cat had been watching from the safety of Jeff the Chalk's front garden, but the sight of those huge dogs had finally got to him. All the cool inside Conkers seemed to drain away. He was like a freezer with the door left open. He was melting! With nerves! He suddenly just wanted to get home. To safety. Away from those dogs. Now. Fast!

So Conkers ran. He ran out of Jeff's garden. He ran on to Pip Street. He ran right under the dogs' noses.

Did the dogs ignore this speeding cat? Did they shrug their doggy shoulders and let Conkers go on his way?

As if!

They were dogs, after all, and dogs are really very famous indeed for NOT liking cats. So they did what any dog would do – they went bananas! All five dogs leaped and pulled, yowling and yelping and chasing after Conkers as he dashed across

the road. The sleigh lurched violently to the side, throwing Walter backwards in his seat and making him drop the reins. The dogs raced after Conkers, and just as Bovver's jaws were about to snap shut on Conkers' tail, the plucky cat leaped on to the wall

alongside Bobby's house and sped into the back garden.

Conkers was safe! But the dogs were not. They were out of control. Bovver swerved to avoid the wall, but he could not stop, and with Walter yelling, "Whoa, whoa," as he bounced about in the back, the crazy sleigh sped off down the pavement then out on to Pip Street and away, the dogs running faster than ever before.

Once Walter was gone, the neighbours turned to Mr Keiths.

"Don't worry, Mr Keiths," piped up Imelda. "Don't look sad and cross and botherated. We can raise the money to fix Pegasus. We can. You try and stop us. Er, actually, don't. Don't stop us. . ."

"Just trust us," Bobby chipped in. "We can do it! We can raise the money and send Walter away once and for all! I know we can!"

"Yes, yes," cried Mrs Rhubarb. "We must fight for you Mr Keiths. And in so doing, we will be fighting for the very future of Pip Street. To battle, dear friends, to battle!"

# 8
# The Big Count Up

The next day was Friday, one of the most popular days of the week. The biscuits had sold out in Café Coffee and round at Bobby's house, the phone was ringing.

"It's Mr Morsel, manager of the Fish Lumps factory here," said the voice belonging to Mr Morsel. "I'm delighted to inform you that Conkers has won the competition. We would like to photograph him right away. Can you come now?"

Bobby agreed. He was so excited his left eyelid started twitching, but luckily he could still see to put Conkers into his basket and rush down to the factory for the photo shoot.

Of course, Conkers was a complete star, posing like a supermodel for his photos, and just two hours later Bobby returned to Pip Street with a cheque for £150 in his pocket.

**Bank of Money**

DATE 01.04.14

PAY Bobby Cobbler

£ 150.00

One hundred and fifty pounds

SIGNED Mr Morsel

123456 00001034180 1000

He was met by all his fellow fundraisers – the Smalls, Dave Pasty, Mrs Rhubarb and Jeff the Chalk.

"We have the money from the biscuit sales at Café Coffee," said Dave, waving a bag of coins.

"And I've just finished my dressing-gown-athon," said Nathan. (Even after several days of solid dressing-gown action, Nathan was still wearing it. Why mess with a good thing?)

"So let's add it all up!" shouted Imelda, excitedly.

Everybody crowded into Bobby's kitchen for The Big Count Up.

"Here is £150 that Conkers won," said Bobby, slapping the cheque on to the table.

Jeff noted it down in his notepad.

"And I should like to contribute something from my personal savings," said Mrs Rhubarb, handing over a £10 note. Then Dave counted the coins from the biscuit sale, which came to £30, and Nathan added up all his sponsorship money, which came to £20. Jeff noted all this down.

"That's, ooh, let me see..." said Imelda. "Oh decapitated coffee! I'm too excited to count. Have we done it? Have we raised £500?"

Jeff shook his head.

"We have raised £210, Imelda," said Nathan, placing a brotherly hand on her shoulder; a shoulder that sagged with the news.

"Not bad, but not enough," said Bobby.

"What are we going to do?" said Imelda, thrusting her tiny hands into her curly red hair.

"I'm not sure," said Bobby, in a serious voice. Everyone fell silent for some seconds, until Bobby spoke again: "We must not lose heart, though. I'm sure we can raise the rest, somehow..." he said.

"Let's at least take the money we have raised to Mr Keiths now."

So the neighbours walked down to Mr Keiths' house. Bobby tapped on the living-room window – Mr Keiths was inside watching the TV programme *Extenders*, about a street in London where people kept adding extra rooms to their houses. Mr Keiths waved and then shuffled to the door, using his stick to steady him.

"Hey people," he said, as he opened it. "What can I do for you all?"

"Good news!" said Bobby. "We have already raised £210 for the **Parts for Pegasus Appeal**. It's yours!"

Bobby handed Mr Keiths the money and the old

guy stood for a moment, looking at it, and then shook his head.

"Thank you," said Mr Keiths. "For everything, but I have been thinking and I reckon Walter is right. I'll never find the rest of the money to fix Pegasus. It's no good. I think it's time I moved in with Tommy."

The neighbours gasped.

"Don't give up, Mr Keiths," said Bobby. "This £210 is a good start. We can raise the rest. And until we do, perhaps you could get Pegasus a little bit fixed?"

"I'm really grateful for the money," added Mr Keiths. "I'll give it to Tommy, for board and lodging. But you guys have done enough now.

This isn't what I wanted or what you wanted, but sometimes in this life, you have to know when to quit."

And with that, Mr Keiths quietly shut the front door and was gone.

# 9
## Clear Outs and Car Boots

The anxious neighbours wandered back on to the street, discussing Mr Keiths' decision and how life on Pip Street would be in trouble if Walter moved in.

"It could mean losing our homes!" said Imelda, looking terrified.

"It would mean destroying that beautiful Pearly Oak tree in Mr Keiths' front garden, too," said

Mrs Rhubarb. "I have always loved that tree. I used to climb it as a girl."

"It would mean no more Mr Keiths," said Bobby.

With a big group sigh, all the neighbours drifted back to their homes, except Bobby, Imelda and Nathan, who stayed outside and talked.

"We can't give up," said Bobby. "Mr Keiths said you have to learn when to quit. But we're not ready to quit, are we? Not yet! We can't let Mr Keiths leave. If we could just raise some more money..."

"I could sell my collection of acorns," said Imelda.

Nathan was about to tell Imelda that sadly, that was not the solution, when Mr Keiths appeared at his front door again and beckoned the children over.

"Don't just stand about looking blue, kids," he said. "If you still want to help me, you can clear out my garage, ready for me to move. But I warn you, it's one big heap of rubbish."

Mr Keiths handed Bobby the garage door key and he unlocked it, then super-tall Nathan pushed the door up – a job he was brilliant at on account of his huge height. Tallness, eh? Very handy for opening garage doors.

The three children gazed, wide-eyed, at what lay inside.

"I've seen some stuff in my time," said Bobby, "but that is a lot of it."

He was right. There was stuff everywhere! Stuff
in boxes. Stuff in piles. Stuff on shelves. Stuff
hanging from the roof. Stuff on top of more stuff,

with stuff poking out of it. And in the middle of it all? Pegasus, of course, parked up and out of action.

Bobby, Imelda and Nathan edged their way inside the garage and began burrowing in all the peculiar odds and ends. They found a plastic bag bulging with old train tickets, a rusty trumpet, two suitcases full of camping magazines and a framed photograph of the Queen riding an elephant.

"Pull it all out on the pavement," called Mr Keiths from his doorstep, "then we can throw it away."

"But this stuff could be worth something," said Bobby, with an excited look on his face and a bright idea in his head. And then: "That's it!" he shouted.

Bobby ran over to Mr Keiths, beaming.

"We'll clear the garage for you Mr Keiths, as long as you let us sell this stuff. There's a car boot sale tomorrow. I saw it advertised in *The Daily Wotsit*," he said. "We might still be able to raise enough to fix Pegasus."

"Ooh, fab idea, Bobbins," said Imelda, while Nathan grinned and nodded. But Mr Keiths was less excited. He shrugged, in a "maybe, possibly, ish" kind of way.

"Don't care what you do with it, it just needs to go," he muttered, before shutting the front door.

The children were not put off by Mr Keiths' lack of enthusiasm. No! They understood that this was their last, best hope; their final chance to save Mr Keiths and keep Walter off Pip Street. They were on a quest. A quest to make £290! A thrilling, noble, car-boot-sale-to-fix-a-mobility-scooter quest. And that's the best kind of quest there is!

# 10
## From Depressed to a Quest

Fired up and full of hope, the children worked for the rest of the day, sorting through the objects in Richard Keiths' garage and piling them up on the pavement, ready for the next day's car boot sale. Bobby's dad had agreed to transport everything to the sale in his car and help the children sell it, too.

They found all kinds of unusual objects from

76

Richard Keiths' past lurking in the garage. There was a box of assorted potato mashers and cheese knives. There were two jackets decorated with sequins, an ice bucket in the shape of a pineapple

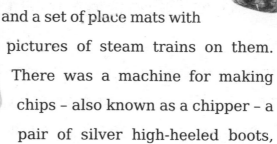

and a set of place mats with pictures of steam trains on them. There was a machine for making chips – also known as a chipper – a pair of silver high-heeled boots, boxes and boxes of old records and a big brown teapot, full to the top with buttons.

It was grubby work – Imelda wore a red scarf around her mouth and nose to keep the dust out and some brown overalls and a flat cap, like an old-fashioned removal man – but the children were happy rummaging, like eager little bunnies on a mission to find chocolate-coated carrots.

By mid-afternoon, Bobby, Imelda and Nathan had almost finished clearing the garage and were taking a break on Mr Keiths' garden wall. Bobby and Imelda were playing Nice Cake or Rice Cake, a game that only they really understood. Bobby had just laid an apricot flapjack card when Mrs Rhubarb emerged from her house. She was carrying some plastic sheeting and two large signs. One read:

## MAKE PEACE NOT GAS!

The other one read

## POPS – PRESERVE OUR PIP STREET!

"What are you doing, Mrs Rhubarb?" asked Bobby.

"I'm going to occupy the Pearly Oak!" she replied, looking fierce. "Walter will not dig it up or chop it down or anything if I'm in it. Call *The Daily Wotsit*, too, and get them to run a story. For now, goodbye!"

The children looked on, amazed, as Mrs Rhubarb strode over to the Pearly Oak outside Mr Keiths' house. She rested her signs against its trunk and threw a rope over a branch. Then, with some difficulty but plenty of determination, she pulled herself up, got comfortable on a branch and opened her backpack. Inside was a box of sandwiches, which Mrs Rhubarb began eating. A few bites into a round of cheese and chutney, she suddenly shouted: "There!"

The children looked up the street and saw Walter sweeping on to it. He raced down the road and as he stopped by the garage, Imelda

sprang up, looking like an angry red squirrel facing down a fat, rude grey squirrel.

"Why the cross face?" asked Walter.

"I am not pleased to see you, Mr Brother of Mr Keiths," said Imelda. "You have caused too much trouble since you first mushed on to this street."

"Well I'm pleased to see you," he said, his slow

smile spreading across his face. "Pleased to see you clearing out the garage, that is. Looks like my brother has finally seen sense and is moving out."

The children said nothing. Mrs Rhubarb lobbed an acorn at Walter. He frowned and looked up.

"Mrs Rhubarb is protesting in the Pearly Oak tree," said Imelda. "She says she won't come down until you leave us alone!"

Walter chuckled quietly.

"A middle-aged actress up a tree is not going to stop me," he said, calmly. "Acorns or no acorns.

You children keep up the good work, now. See you very soon!"

Then Walter shouted

"MUSH!" and the dogs sped away, leaving trails of dribble down the middle of the street, as proof they had been there.

Mrs Rhubarb swung down from the tree using the rope-and-pulley system she had hooked up to make receiving supplies easier and offered Imelda, who was fuming, the rest of her sandwich. Bobby put a reassuring arm around his small friend's shoulder.

"Don't let him upset you," said Bobby, kindly.

Everyone stood quietly for a few seconds, before Bobby reminded them that they had a job to do.

"Come on," he said. "The car boot sale is tomorrow and we need to be ready."

"Why yes!" said Mrs Rhubarb. "And just look

at the treasures you have uncovered. How marvellous! Place mats and jackets and, well, many other wonderful items. Surely, they will sell for a fortune!"

The children were not sure, but they had to try. Bobby nodded at Nathan and Imelda and the three of them, looking determined, piled back into the garage

# 11
## Car Boot Loot

Bobby, Imelda and Nathan worked into the evening, clearing out every last box and bag and suitcase from Mr Keiths' garage, and then rose early the next day for the car boot sale. They unpacked Mr Keiths' oddments from the car and laid them all out on a big table. Immediately, people crowded around the goodies, like a swarm of locusts on a shopping trip. The sparkly jackets went quickly and fetched £20 each. The boots raised £10. One old lady, wearing a brightly coloured poncho and green wellies, seemed very excited to find the teapot full of buttons.

"Ooh, buttons, buttons, lovely buttons," she cooed, happily handing over £5 for the lot.

This was great. The children felt excited. Sales came thick and fast and their pot of money grew and grew. Mr Cobbler bought the children bacon sarnies to congratulate them, and they munched happily, chatting about how much they had raised and feeling sure it would be enough. But as the morning wore on, people got over their junk excitement and sales dried up. No one wanted to

buy the Donny Chopsticks calendar from 1973, or the trumpet, or the mouldy hammock, or a book about chickens.

At midday, the children packed up and returned to Bobby's house. Sitting around the kitchen table, Nathan and Bobby carefully sorted all the coins and notes, while Imelda paced nervously. There seemed to be heaps of money, but once it had all been counted up the total came to just £73. It was good, but it was not enough to mend Pegasus.

Bobby and Nathan sighed, but Imelda felt so cross and disappointed and worried 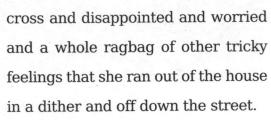 and a whole ragbag of other tricky feelings that she ran out of the house in a dither and off down the street.

Mr Keiths spotted her. He was sitting in his front garden again.

"What's up, short stuff?" he cried and Imelda stopped, but could not speak.

Bobby and Nathan caught up with Imelda and

the three children went to see Mr Keiths.

"I'm glad you're here. I need to tell you that I'm off tomorrow," said Mr Keiths. "Tommy's helping move my stuff. It's time. I'm leaving Pip Street."

"Oh, Mr K," Imelda sobbed. "We tried, we really did. All those biscuits and the cat beauty contest and the car boot sale..."

"I know," said Mr Keiths, "but what can't be helped, can't be helped, you know? It didn't work out for me and Pegasus, but you know what? It's OK, because I have you people. You children tried so hard for me, raising money and clearing the garage. Wow! That blew me away! It's riches to me."

The children sighed. It was a lovely sentiment and surprising, too – Mr Keiths wasn't usually so affectionate. They all hugged him quietly.

"I will still stand up to Walter," Mrs Rhubarb shouted from the tree. "Even if you leave, Mr Keiths, I can stay in the tree and try to stop him knocking down our street."

But Mr Keiths just smiled doubtfully. He knew Walter was a very hard man to beat.

"Oh, I almost forgot," Bobby said, and he nipped into the garage and then returned, carrying a box. "There was one last box in there.

It is full of old letters. We thought you might want to keep them."

Then the children plodded home. Oh dear. Poor them. And poor Mr Keiths. And poor Pip Street. Was there any hope? Any help? Any anything? I don't know, but I know a chapter that does. . . The next one!

# 12
## So, Farewell Then. . .

By the time Bobby, Imelda and Nathan woke up the next day, Mrs Rhubarb was up in the tree again and Tommy was already loading boxes from Mr Keiths' house into his white van. The children went to help.

They lifted and loaded all morning, and then at lunchtime the sound of sleigh bells drew a sigh from the packers and a rustle from Mrs Rhubarb.

Walter pulled up by Mr Keiths' house. He looked at the children and the boxes and smiled. "Well, well," he said. "Richard Montgomery Banjo Keiths is leaving at last."

Mr Keiths shuffled over to the sleigh, with his stick supporting him, to speak to his brother.

"I'll be gone by tonight," he said quietly. "This street and these people have been good to me, Walter. I hope you're good to them, too."

"Oh certainly!" said Walter. "If – *when* – I find gas, I will make sure everyone moves out, so I can dig Pip Street up completely! I'll be doing everybody a favour, really. Giving them a chance to start a new life somewhere else. I don't see why you're all so fond of this street anyway!"

"Shame on you," shouted Mrs Rhubarb from the Pearly Oak, throwing some more acorns at him, but Walter took no notice. He just smiled and mushed away.

With a heavy heart, Bobby and the children carried on

working, and by the afternoon, the last load was packed into the van and Tommy drove away with it.

"Reckon that's the lot," Mr Keiths said. "Apart from that last box of old letters. I've still got time to sort through them before Tommy comes back to collect me."

The children nodded silently.

Richard Keiths shook Nathan's hand and then hugged Bobby gently. Then he turned to Imelda, who was upset but also cross, and didn't know whether to cry or frown or both.

"I want you to have this," Mr Keiths said, patting Imelda's red curls. "I found it in my mum's old chest of drawers."

Mr Keiths handed Imelda a small drawstring bag.

"Now I think I'll have a few minutes in the old place alone," he said, pointing at his house. "Before Tommy comes to get me."

And that was that. Mr Keiths returned to his house – the house he had loved so much and lived in for so long – for the very last time.

# 13
## Beeches and Brooches

Feeling super-extra-double-triple-sad, Imelda, Nathan and Bobby went back to Bobby's house.

"*How Much?* is on soon," said Bobby. "We could watch it. For old time's sake."

Imelda nodded quietly and the three friends settled on the sofa.

As the *How Much?* music began, Imelda opened her drawstring bag. Inside was a gorgeous

 brooch, made of twisty metal with a gem in the centre. The metal was faded and the gem was dull, but it was still a lovely thing. Imelda showed it to Bobby and Nathan.

"Nice," said Bobby, pinning it on to her jumper.

"It's started," said Nathan, pointing at the TV as the *How Much?* opening music played.

The children watched in silence. There were no explosions of "How much?" No giddy laughter. They just let it wash over their tired, miserable minds.

Which is why, halfway through the programme, none of them recognized the brooch that was being examined. A silver brooch with a single sapphire in the middle. Carshalton Beeches, the expert, had been talking about it for some time when suddenly. . .

"Wait a second!" said Bobby, sitting forward like he'd been poked with a sharpened runner bean. "Imelda, show us your brooch again."

Imelda quickly took it off her jumper and held it up. The children stared from her brooch to the one on the screen.

"It's an exact match," shouted Imelda.

"Yes!" said Bobby. "Now listen. He's about to say how much."

On the TV, Carshalton Beeches stared at the brooch.

"I should say this beautiful object is worth in the region of. . ."

He paused.

"Something along the lines of. . ."

He paused again.

"Well, it's difficult to say," he said.

"COME ON BEECHES!" Imelda shouted at the screen. "DISH IT!"

"As a rough estimate," Carshalton Beeches

finally said, "I would think this brooch is worth about £300!"

# "HOW MUCH?"

shouted the children, jumping up at once.

They could not believe their eyes or ears or faces! Forget rusty trumpets and out-of-date calendars, here was something that actually had some value! The brooch! And if they added the £300 it was worth together with the money they had already raised it made more than enough to buy the parts for Pegasus.

Bobby, Imelda and Nathan danced and hugged, but there was no time to savour this delicious, unexpected victory. . .

"We have to stop Mr Keiths," said Bobby, suddenly. "We have to tell him there is enough money now!"

"But he's leaving," shouted Imelda. "Tonight. This evening. *Now*!"

# 14
## Follow That Van!

Imelda was right. Mr Keiths was so close to leaving Pip Street, he had practically left it.

Tommy had helped his grandfather into the van and was just driving up Pip Street as the children dashed outside. Too late! The van whizzed past Bobby's house, music thumping from its stereo.

"Stop, stop!" yelled Imelda, running up the pavement.

It was no use. The van turned the corner and disappeared.

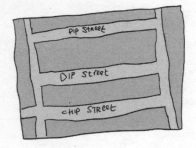

"Come on," said Bobby. "We can head it off at the top of Dip Street. Let's take the shortcut through your garden."

The children raced through the Smalls' house, into the garden and through a gap in the hedge, then out on to Dip Street. At the top of the street, the children looked for the van.

"There!" said Nathan, pointing.

The van had stopped at the zebra crossing nearby, to allow a party of nuns returning to St Winnipop's Convent to cross the road.

"Let's go!" shouted Imelda, running towards the van.

But the children were soon stopped in their tracks. A moving wall of nuns advanced towards them, blocking the pavement and engulfing our friends.

"Ahh," cried Imelda, who was lost in the crowd. "Don't like it. I'm cluster-phobic!"

Behind her, Bobby was stuck too and, being a polite boy, he did not want to shove or push. Besides, you cannot shove a nun – that's an absolute rule for life. Instead, he stood still while the nuns, in their black robes, surged slowly around him. Only Nathan – tall, tall Nathan – could see what was happening.

"The van's coming!" Nathan yelled.

Imelda and Bobby tried to hop up and down, but they were blocked in. So Nathan did the only thing he could think to do. He picked up Imelda, plucking her from the river of nuns like a fisherman netting a trout, and plonked her on his shoulders.

Surely, Tommy and Mr Keiths could not miss a giant with a tiny, shouting pixie on his shoulders? A pixie with red hair that shone out like a beacon and little arms that waved madly?

"Here it comes," shouted Imelda.

The van was speeding up. Music was still pounding from its stereo.

"They are not going to see us," said Nathan. "They're not looking our way. What can we do?"

Imelda ripped off the red scarf she was wearing around her neck and waved it furiously just as Bobby managed to wriggle out from within the crowd of nuns, and made it to the edge of the pavement.

The van thundered towards them. Bobby glanced up at Imelda – and had an idea!

"Throw it, Imelda," Bobby shouted. "Throw the scarf! Aim for the windscreen. Do it! Now!"

Imelda threw the scarf,

which unfurled in the sky like a crimson streamer and then floated down, right on to the windscreen of the van, blocking Tommy's view. Tommy slammed on the brakes and, as the van screeched to a halt, Mr Keiths finally saw the children out of his window, huddled excitedly on the pavement. He wound down the window, with a "what's going on?" look on his lined old face.

"What is it, kids?" Mr Keiths asked. "This better be good. I need to get going."

"It is good! Really good!" said Bobby, panting. "That brooch you gave to Imelda was on *How Much?* just now. An exact same one."

"So?" said Mr Keiths.

"So?" gasped Bobby. "It's only worth £300, isn't it?"

"How much?" said Richard Keiths *and* all the nuns, at exactly the same time.

"It's enough for parts for Pegasus," said Imelda, clambering down from Nathan's shoulders. "You don't need to leave Pip Street, Mr Keiths."

"We did it!" said Bobby, grinning. "We raised the money. You're saved!"

# 15
## All Back to Pip Street

I hardly need describe the scenes of joy that followed. But I will anyway.

Tommy drove Mr Keiths back to Pip Street, with music blaring from the van's stereo. Nathan, Imelda and Bobby ran along behind, cheering, and the nuns followed after, chattering excitedly. Never had such a procession been seen before, and let's face it, Pip Street has seen some pretty odd events over the years, so that's saying something.

The neighbours left their houses and joined the celebrations. Jeff the Chalk chalked pictures of fireworks and champagne on the pavement, which really helped the party mood. The Cobblers hugged their son, little Dave Pasty did a little Pasty jig and Trevor Scribe from *The Daily Wotsit,* who had been photographing Mrs Rhubarb's tree protest, now took pictures of the party procession.

It was a joyful scene, but short-lived because cutting through the cheers and laughter came the dreaded sound of sleigh bells.

Walter William Keiths drove on to Pip Street in his crazy sleigh, a cigar lolling from his mouth. He

looked pleased with himself at first, imagining that his brother's house was now his, but the cigar tumbled from Walter's mouth when he saw the crowd.

"WHOA," he shouted, stopping the dogs just in time to avoid a terrible nun-dog-neighbour pile-up.

"I presume you are just leaving, brother," said Walter. "Which means the house is mine."

"You presume wrong," said Mr Keiths. Tommy

114

had helped him out of the van and he stood leaning on his stick calmly to face his bothersome brother. "Thanks to my pals here, I now have enough money to fix Pegasus. I won't be leaving Pip Street any time soon."

"Nonsense!" exploded Walter, heaving himself down from the sleigh and limping over to his brother. "You're lying. It's a lie. Don't lie. I don't take kindly to lies or liars."

"It's all true," said Bobby. "We worked as a team and raised enough money."

"So why don't you just hop it, Mr Moustache Man with your malamute mutts?" shouted Imelda, feeling bold.

Walter stared coldly at the crowd then very

slowly climbed back into his sleigh. But, being Walter, he had to have the last word, didn't he?

"It's very nice that you have rescued my brother *this time*," he said, picking up the reins and then staring at everyone again. "But what happens when Pegasus breaks down *next time*? I'll tell you what happens..."

"No, you won't," said Mr Keiths. "I will tell *you* what happens. I found this when the garage was cleared out."

Mr Keiths took a crumpled sheet of paper from his pocket, with fine, swirly handwriting on it.

"It's from Tabitha Keiths – our mum. It says the house is mine, for ever and always, to do with as I like. Mine – you understand? There is nothing in this letter about you getting the house. You don't get it if Pegasus breaks down again, Walter. You don't get it when I leave, either. You don't get it ever."

The Pip Street people cheered and then quickly fell silent as Richard Keiths went on.

"You have been lying to me all these years," said Mr Keiths. "But I have found you out, and now I want you to go, brother."

117

"Bravo!" came a shout from the Pearly Oak tree. "Quite so – out with you!"

The crowd looked up. Mrs Rhubarb pushed some leaves apart and popped her head out.

"I have had enough of your threats and devilish plans to ruin our beautiful street, Walter Keiths," she said. "It will be my pleasure to escort you from this neighbourhood once and most certainly for all."

Walter just smirked, as if to say "Please! You?" but his smirk disappeared when, with a huge rustle of leaves, Mrs Rhubarb swung down from the tree using her ropes and pulleys and landed – BLAM! – in Walter's sleigh, like an awesome lady Rhubarb ninja.

Before Walter could protest, Mrs Rhubarb grabbed a tuna and sweetcorn sandwich from her backpack and used it to cuff Walter around his moustached chops. Then she seized the reins and, with a loud MUSH in her finest actor voice, sent Viper, Storm, Clamp, Bovver and Reggie hurtling off down Pip Street.

The neighbours and nuns stared after the speeding sleigh in disbelief.

"Will she be all right?" asked Bobby, as the sleigh sped around the corner with photographer Trevor Scribe from *The Daily Wotsit* in hot pursuit, snapping pictures.

"Sure," said Mr Keiths. "Mrs Rhubarb is large and in charge! She isn't a woman to be messed with when her blood's up. I believe Walter has met his match here on Pip Street. It's victory to us! Sweet!"

# 16
## All's Well That Ends Well

So Walter William Keiths was sent packing, once and for all. Mrs Rhubarb returned a few hours later. She would not say where she had been or what she had seen or done, but she had a triumphant look in her eye. Walter had been defeated and, with the money to fix Pegasus and proof that he owned his Pip Street home, Mr Keiths was finally safe.

So it was that Richard Keiths stayed on Pip Street. He sold the precious brooch and Tommy bought all the new parts and fixed Pegasus. Then the neighbours gathered to watch Mr Keiths climb into his newly repaired mobility scooter and rev her up for a celebratory spin to the Co-op.

"Sure feels good to have the old girl running again," said Mr Keiths. "All thanks to you children and to you, Mrs Rhubarb! And to Conkers – I'm going to buy you some packets of Fish Lumps with your face on them!" Conkers miaowed, proudly.

"But before I hit the Co-op, I think it's time you kids had a treat," said Mr Keiths, looking at Bobby, Imelda and Nathan. "How about a slap-up breakfast at Café Coffee? There is a little cash left over from your fundraising and I want to spend it on you, to say thanks."

124

"Are you sure?" said Bobby.

"Of course he's sure," said Imelda. "Yippee! You're the best, Mr K!"

"How about double waffles and hot chocolate with extra marshmallows?" said Mr Keiths, revving Pegasus. "Sound good? Come on then kids, race you!"

With that, Mr Keiths shot off down Pip Street on Pegasus and with a group "Whoop!" Bobby, Imelda and Nathan took off after him, laughing and shrieking as they ran.

TURN OVER
FOR MORE

FUN

# QUIZ TIME

Which of these things did Bobby, Imelda and Nathan find in Richard Keiths' garage?

a) An ice bucket shaped like a pineapple

b) A live tiger

c) A machine for making sausages

d) Two jackets decorated with sequins

e) A book about chickens

f) A teapot shaped like Elvis

g) A bucket filled with cheese

# The Daily Wotsit

From time to time, Bobby's local paper, *The Daily Wotsit*, covers some really big and important stories. Here are a selection of headlines from "scoops" of the past:

**SHOCKING NEW MEDICAL RESEARCH SUGGESTS: SWEETS ARE BAD FOR YOUR TEETH**

**LOCAL TREES "DANGEROUSLY LEAFY" WARNS VISITING SCIENTIST**

**OUT OF CONTROL SATELLITE TO CRASH LAND ON PIP STREET – POSSIBLY**

**WOMAN WHO PICKED UP WRONG CHILD FROM SCHOOL APOLOGIZES TO HEAD TEACHER**

**LOCAL FAT MAN MISTAKEN FOR PRIZE PUMPKIN AT VILLAGE SHOW – FULL REPORT INSIDE**

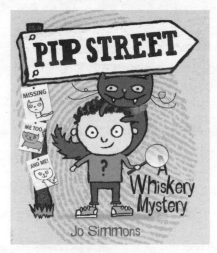

Have you seen Bobby Cobbler's cat, Conkers?
He looks like a miniature black panther (on a good day).

But Conkers is nowhere to be found.
He's not on Pip Street!

He's disappeared – along with lots of other cats.
What in the name of frying pans is going on?

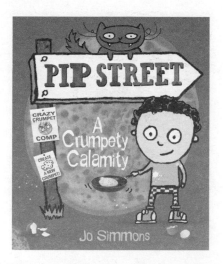

Ahoy there! Do you like crumpets?
Well, not many people on Pip Street do,
which is why Bobby Cobbler's dad, head of
the local crumpet factory, is throwing a taste-tastic
crumpet competition — to make them more
scrumptious and exciting!

Who will win? Who will come last? And who borrowed
my blue pen? (I'd like it back, please.)

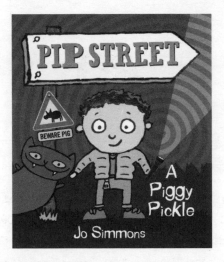

A plague of power cuts has hit Pip Street,
which is bad news for usually brave
Bobby Cobbler. He's scared of the dark!

Can Bobby's top chum Imelda help
him fight his fear? Can our two friends
restore power to Pip Street?

Jo Simmons lives in Brighton with her husband and two children. They share their home with a dog called Betty and a cat called Pickle (before you ask – no, they don't get on. Pickle lives upstairs; Betty lives downstairs).

Jo likes sleeping, running and eating ice cream straight from the pot, though not all at the same time, of course. That would be silly. And impossible.

**www.visitpipstreet.com**

Steve Wells is a designer and illustrator. As a child,
he spent all his time drawing cartoons and at weekends he
would travel around London looking for interesting books
and comics. Now he designs books and book covers for
a living – he has illustrated fourteen books and designed
more than 150 so far. Steve lives in Bath with his
wife and three children, a cat and a lizard

**www.visitpipstreet.com**